For Maria Baghramian and Hormoz Farhat.
And, of course, for the spirit of Saadi.
—D.J.N.

For Ann Neuman
—J.L.

Text copyright © 2013 by Donna Jo Napoli
Illustrations copyright © 2013 by Jim LaMarche

First Edition
1 3 5 7 9 10 8 6 4 2
H106-9333-5-5-13074

Printed in Malaysia

This story was loosely inspired by a medieval Persian poem from *The Gulistan* of Sa'di.

The art was created with acrylic paint and colored pencils on Arches hotpress watercolor paper.
Designed by Tanya Ross-Hughes

Library of Congress Cataloging-in-Publication Data

Napoli, Donna Jo, 1948–
  A single pearl / by Donna Jo Napoli ; illustrated by Jim LaMarche.—First edition.
    pages cm
  Summary: "A simple grain of sand undergoes an inspiring transformation"—Provided by publisher.
  ISBN 978-1-4231-4557-8—ISBN 1-4231-4557-7
  [1. Sand—Fiction. 2. Pearls—Fiction. 3. Metamorphosis—Fiction.] I. LaMarche, Jim, illustrator. II. Title.
  PZ7.N15Shr 2013
    [E]—dc23   2012032398

Reinforced binding
Visit www.disneyhyperionbooks.com

A Single Pearl

By Donna Jo Napoli

Illustrated by Jim LaMarche

DISNEY · HYPERION BOOKS
NEW YORK

A grain of sand
fell into the ocean
past so many creatures
to the very bottom,
where sand went out in every direction
for what seemed like forever
to the grain of sand.

"The ocean bed is huge and important,"
said the grain of sand. "In comparison,
I don't matter at all. I am worthless."

The grain of sand would have cried,
if sand could make tears.

A hungry oyster
drew water through its gills,
stirring up the ocean bed,
filtering out its food from the floating seaweed.

The grain of sand got stuck
between the oyster's mantle and shell
and struggled at first to get free.
Then it gave up the struggle,
for, after all, what did it matter?
It was only a single grain of sand.

The grain of sand would have curled in despair,
if sand could curl.

But that single grain
in that very spot
irritated the poor oyster,
who protected itself
by coating the sand with a shiny layer
year after year.

The grain of sand felt more and more alone and lost.

One day, a daring diver
put on a nose clip and finger guards
and climbed onto a weighted bar
so his friend could lower him
into the cold sea.

He dug up the oyster
and put it into his net basket.

When the diver got back on land, he pried open the shell
and gasped at the glorious pearl.
He quickly put it in his pocket.
The grain of sand was overcome
by all the rapid changes—
from inside the cold oyster
to out in the hot sun
to deep in the dark pocket.

The grain of sand would have shivered with dread,
if sand could shiver.

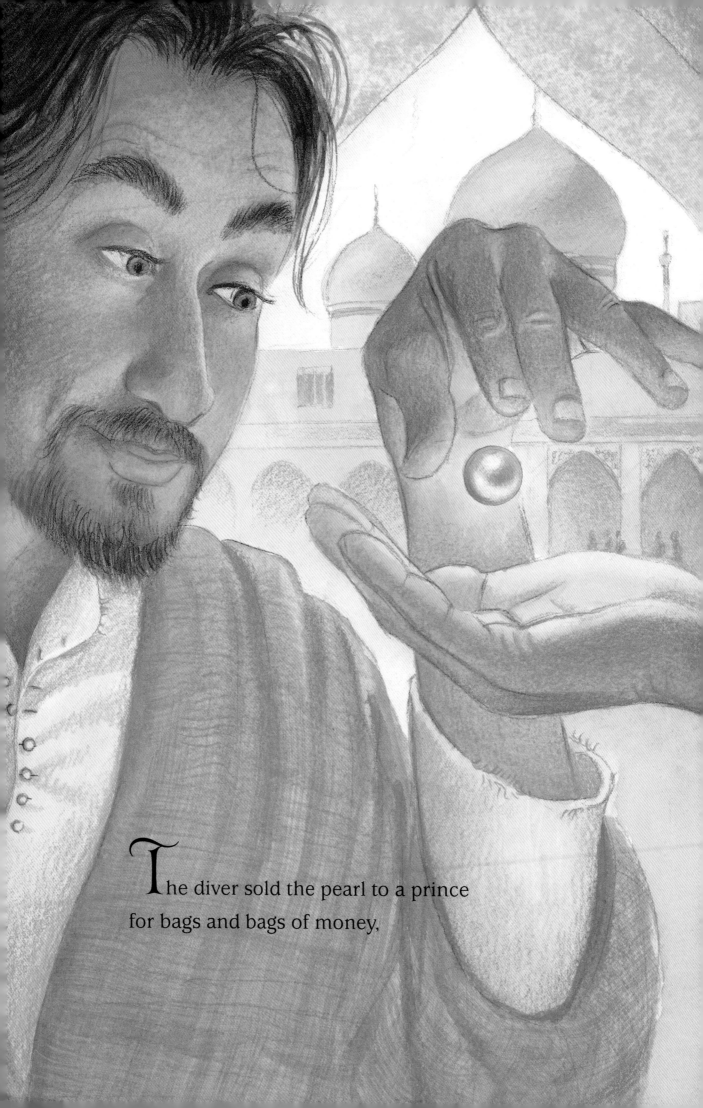

The diver sold the pearl to a prince
for bags and bags of money,

The prince, in turn, gave it to his beloved wife, who said it glowed like the moon.

She saved it on a slip
of velvet in a gold cup
until she had a daughter
whose laughter was as light
and whose face was as lovely
as the moon.

For the third time, the pearl changed hands.
The young princess hung it around her neck
and held it tenderly.
The grain of sand felt her warmth and love.
This was where it was supposed to be.
This was home.

The grain of sand laughed in joy, for anyone can laugh.

It was so admired that pearls became
the imperial jewel of choice in all Persia.

The grain of sand sat
in the center of the pearl.
And it mattered.